The Tiny Explorers

Kat Macleod

T&H

One afternoon in a busy garden,
the Tiny Explorers are searching for treasure.

Through the towers of grass
where the light doesn't reach ...

What's this?

A juicy blueberry.

Past the forest of flowers
craning their necks ...

What's this?

A velvety feather.

Under the daisies
and dandelion clocks ...

What's this?

A glossy acorn.

Around the mushrooms
arranged in a ring ...

What's this?

A bumpy seedpod.

Between the roses
with prickly stems ...

What's this?

A silky ribbon.

Over the lily pads
afloat on the pond ...

What's this?

A glimmering coin.

Into the cave
tucked between rocks ...

What's this!

Can you spot
all the treasures
at the Tiny Explorers' party?

For Jimmy, Abe & Winnie,
my tiny explorers.

Kat Macleod is an illustrator, designer and exhibiting artist. She is endlessly inspired by nature, fashion and textiles, and the drawings of her three young boys.

First published in Australia in 2021
by Thames & Hudson Australia Pty Ltd
11 Central Boulevard, Portside Business Park
Port Melbourne, Victoria 3207
ABN: 72 004 751 964

thamesandhudson.com.au

24 23 22 21 5 4 3 2 1

Thames & Hudson Australia and the author wish to acknowledge that Aboriginal and Torres Strait Islander people are the traditional custodians of this land where we live, learn, work and play.

ISBN 978-1-760-76115-8

A catalogue record for this book is available from the National Library of Australia

Design: Kat Macleod
Printed and bound in China by 1010 Printing International Limited

FSC® is dedicated to the promotion of responsible forest management worldwide.
This book is made of material from FSC®-certified forests and other controlled sources.

Kat Macleod